Jane Hissey
RUFF

Random House New York

Old Bear, Bramwell Brown, and Little Bear had stopped to listen to a strange noise.

"It's something outside the door saying 'ruff, ruff,'" said Old Bear. "I think I'd better take a look."

Old Bear carefully opened the door, and in bounced a woolly
dog. The dog almost knocked Little Bear off his feet, but
Duck caught him just in time.

"Hello," said Old Bear. "Who are you?"

"I'm a dog," said their visitor.

"We guessed that," said Little Bear, straightening his trousers.
"But what's your name?"

"I don't think I've got one," said the dog, trying to look at his collar while bouncing on Duck's toes.

"We could call you Ruff," said Little Bear. "Old Bear said he heard a ruff outside."

"I like that," said the dog. "Does everyone here have a name?"

"I think so," said Little Bear, and he took Ruff to meet the other toys.

"Do you all live here?" asked Ruff.
"Yes," said Duck. "Where do you live?"
"I don't know," said Ruff. "I was left in the garden next door. I don't think anyone really wants me."
"I wonder why," muttered Duck, looking at the muddy footprints Ruff had left all over the floor.

"Perhaps it was because I was rather bouncy," said Ruff. "When I was younger," he added quickly.

"You still are," grumbled Duck.

Ruff sat down quickly to keep his paws still.

"Everyone's bouncy when they're young," said Little Bear kindly. "How old are you now, Ruff?"

Ruff counted his paws. "One, two, three, four." Then he added his ears. "Five, six." And finally his nose. "Seven," he said. "I think I'm seven."

"Don't you *know?*" said Little Bear. "I always count my *birthdays*."

Ruff said that was a good idea. But since he'd never had a birthday, there was nothing to count.

"Never had a birthday?" chorused the others. "Why not?"

"Nobody ever gave me one," said Ruff.

"That's dreadful," said Little Bear. "Old Bear has had hundreds."

"If you can stay the night with us," said Bramwell Brown, "we'll give you a birthday tomorrow."

"Better still," said Old Bear, "we'll give Ruff *seven* birthdays—one for each year he's missed."

"An all-week birthday," said Rabbit. "Whoopee!"

"Does that mean I can stay for seven nights?" asked Ruff hopefully.

"Of course," said Old Bear. "And you can sleep on our bed if you like."

"As long as you don't bounce," said Duck.

The next day was Monday. It was Ruff's first birthday.

"Happy birthday, Ruff!" cried all the toys as he jumped down from the bed.

He was soon wearing a special birthday bow Little Bear gave him.

The others gave him presents, too—a rubber bone, a new collar, two pairs of boots, and three balls.

Bramwell Brown had made a beautiful birthday cake.

"That smells delicious," said Ruff. But he sniffed just a little too closely, and some of the icing stuck to his nose.

"*Ah-tish-ooo!*" He sneezed so hard that he blew out the candle on his cake. The others thought he meant to blow it out, so they all sang "Happy birthday to Ruff."

It's nice to have friends to share a cake with, thought Ruff.

On Tuesday it was Ruff's second birthday.

"Let's play Treasure Hunt with Ruff's birthday presents," suggested Little Bear.

Ruff wasn't sure that was a good idea.

"Couldn't we use something else for treasure?" he asked. "I haven't had my presents very long."

"I'll just hide the three balls then," said Little Bear.

It was great fun hunting for treasure, and they quickly found two of the balls. But nobody could find the third one. It was only when Little Bear discovered he couldn't sit down for tea that he remembered he'd hidden it in his trousers.

"I thought they were a bit lumpy," he said.

Ruff's cake had two candles on it. He blew them out very carefully.

Only five days to go, he thought sadly. *I wish I could stay longer.*

On Wednesday it was Ruff's third birthday.
All his new friends gave him cards they had made themselves. Ruff read them over and over again—the right way up, upside down, inside out, and back to front. Then he put them in a row to admire them all together.

Zebra arrived with Ruff's birthday cake. "Are you ready to blow out your candles?" she said.

Ruff took a deep breath and blew. *"Whoooooooo!"*

Out went the candles…and down went the cards.

What a lot of cards! thought Ruff happily. *That's how many friends I have.* And he propped them up all over again.

On Thursday it was Ruff's fourth birthday.

"We'll play Musical Chairs," said Old Bear. "Only, we'll use cushions."

"Mmm, cushions are better for bouncing on than chairs," said Ruff, testing them one by one.

Duck quickly moved out of the way. "I think I'd rather play the music," he said.

When he stopped playing, everyone sat on a cushion—except for Ruff, who landed on Rabbit by mistake.

"I think you're out, Ruff," said Little Bear. But they let him play to the end of the game anyway because it was his birthday.

Ruff had only enough puff to blow out three of the candles on his cake. But he wagged his tail so hard that the last one went out, too.

You can never have as much fun as this on your own, thought Ruff.

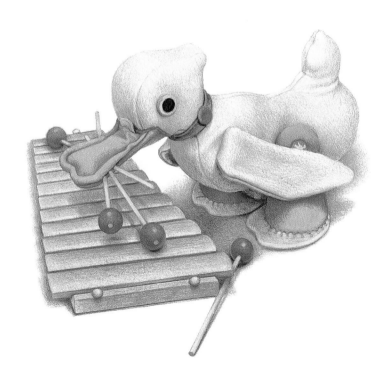

On Friday it was Ruff's fifth birthday.
"I thought we could play Pass the Package today," said Old Bear.
He showed the toys a huge lumpy bundle he had wrapped up specially.

The toys sat in a circle and passed the package round and round.
When the music stopped, the one holding the package peeled off a
layer of paper.

But when it was Ruff's turn, he was so excited he tore off *all* the
paper to reach the prize in the middle.

"That was not playing properly," said Old Bear.
Ruff's tail drooped. "I'm sorry," he said. And to show
just how sorry he was, he let everyone play with his prize *and*
blow out the candles on his cake.

"Can I still have another birthday tomorrow?" he asked.
"Of course," said Old Bear. "But try to be good."

On Saturday it was Ruff's sixth birthday.
He tried to be very good. He blew up lots of balloons and hardly
bounced at all.

Old Bear couldn't think of any more games, so they asked Ruff what
he would like to do.

"Well, I've always wanted to drive a train," he said.

The little wooden train in the nursery was too small to carry everyone.
So they made a bigger train out of cardboard boxes and string.

"All aboard!" cried Ruff, jumping in. He was in such a hurry to drive
off that he nearly forgot Little Bear.

When the train stopped, they all had a piece of Ruff's birthday cake. Ruff counted the candles. "One, two, three, four, five, six…Oh, dear," he sighed.

"What's the matter?" asked Little Bear.

"Tomorrow will be my last birthday," said Ruff sadly.

"Not really," said Old Bear. "After tomorrow you'll have one birthday every year. Just like the rest of us."

It would be nice to be like everyone else, thought Ruff.

On Sunday it was Ruff's seventh birthday.
But when he woke up, there was nobody there.

"Perhaps they've all forgotten me," he sighed. "Or maybe they want me to go now."

Sadly, he gathered up his new collar, his rubber bone, and the three balls. He wrote a note saying "Thank you for a lovely time. Love, Ruff."

He put on his shiny new boots and went to the door. It was then he heard a strange noise out in the hall. He opened the door a crack and peeped outside. There were all his friends!

"Surprise, surprise!" they said. "Happy birthday, Ruff! We have a special present for you." And they brought in a beautiful cushion decorated with Ruff's favorite things.

"We'd like you to stay with us, Ruff. This is your very own place to sleep," said Little Bear.

"Oh, thank you!" said Ruff, jumping right into the middle of his present. "Now that this is my new home, I'll be able to give *you* birthday surprises, too."

And they all agreed that Ruff's seventh birthday was the happiest one of all.

For James

"Ruff" birthday cards designed by Alison Hissey

First American Edition, 1994.
Copyright © 1994 by Jane Hissey. All rights reserved under International and Pan-American Copyright Conventions. Published in the United States of America by Random House, Inc., New York. Originally published in Great Britain by Hutchinson Children's Books Ltd., London, in 1994.
Library of Congress Cataloging-in-Publication Data
Hissey, Jane.
Ruff / Jane Hissey. p. cm. SUMMARY: No one has ever cared enough to have a birthday party for a woolly dog, until he is taken in by some other toys, who give him not one but seven parties.
ISBN 0-679-86042-8 [1. Toys—Fiction. 2. Birthdays—Fiction. 3. Parties—Fiction.] I. Title.
PZ7. H627Ru 1994 [E]—dc20 93-48613

Manufactured in Singapore 10 9 8 7 6 5 4 3 2 1

Random House, Inc. New York, Toronto, London, Sydney, Auckland